JoJo & MoMo's Awesome Adventures:
Big Bear Lake

HEMAL RAJESH SHAH

Acknowledgements

To Jinay, Devyaan, Eva, MoMo, and JoJo, our little angels.

To my parents, Rajesh and Vina, and my sister Pari, for the wonderful childhood & memories.

To my wife Mansi, for the everlasting love & support.

To Mother Nature, for the endless inspiration & energy.

Who, Why, What, Where, Woohoo!

Hi! I am JoJo, a Shih-Poo pup. I have boundless love & energy, and live life fast, can you keep up?

Hello, I am MoMo, an African Leopard Tortoise, and JoJo's older brother. I like my peace & quiet, and live life slow, going with the flow y'know.

Being outdoors and exploring mother nature is so much fun! Away from screens, in the fresh air and under the happy Sun!

So our parents are sending us on an adventure, to Big Bear Lake in California, are you ready to join us?!

Yes, yes, let's get our foot out the door, and see where the road takes us!

Are you a JoJo, a MoMo, or both?

JoJo & MoMo have their own way of enjoying the outdoors!

JoJo the Pup loves to do the fast & exciting activities when being out, while MoMo the Tort loves to do the slow & relaxing ones.

Being "a JoJo" will make your mind & heart race with joy!

Being "a MoMo" will keep you calm, cozy, and equally happy!

At Big Bear Lake, you can be either "a JoJo" or "a MoMo," so come, friend, make your pick or be both, there's no right or wrong, only fun, fun, fun!

Pack our stuff, and off we go!

Packing for a trip is an
important skill.
Pack light, pack smart,
never overfill!

Can you tell what all things are
JoJo and MoMo packing for their
trip to Big Bear Lake? Some are
common to both, some are
unique to each!

JoJo On the Mountains

"MoMo look, we're finally here, and there's so much to do! So without much further ado..."

JoJo jumps on a ski-lift, straight to the top of Bear Mountain, oh what a view! He starts zooming around on fresh powder, with the wind in his face, tongue out loose, barking ever louder!

Oh, he could go on all morning, whether it be sledding, skiing or snowboarding!

MoMo On the Mountains

MoMo happily crawls into a quiet Gondola instead, content to meet JoJo later. "It's a beautiful day out and everyone's merry, so what's the hurry?"

Once on top, MoMo enjoys a hot coffee, takes in the view, stretches out in the sun (snow angels!), and takes in some more of that gorgeous view.

"What have we here, a little cave in the snow? How nice, just a large enough gap, let me squeeze in for a quick nap (....zzzzzzzzzzz)."

JoJo In the Forest

JoJo had a blast in the snow, but he's just getting started! "MoMo, come, a forest awaits below the snow line. More fun under the sun, oh we're so not done!"

A quick snack, a quick drink, a quick rest, and off goes JoJo!

"This forest is so inviting, so I will explore it as much as I can, whether it be bouldering, ziplining, or mountain biking. Woof-woof-wooooof!"

MoMo In the Forest

MoMo chose to explore the forest with a casual stroll in its cool shade, surrounded by sweet sounds of birds chirping and leaves rustling in the gentle breeze.

"Oh, I could do this all week," said MoMo, "watching the birds and butterflies, foraging for my lunch, and napping by this lovely creek."

JoJo On the Lake

"Wow, mother nature never ceases to amaze," says JoJo, "the mighty mountains, fluffy forests and now this lake, in all its vastness and shiny glaze!"

JoJo wasted no time enjoying Big Bear Lake his way. "MoMo you drive!" said JoJo, throwing the motorboat's keys to him. And off went JoJo for the next couple of hours, wakeboarding, wakeskating, waketubing and waterskiing! Woof-Woof-Weeeee!

MoMo On the Lake

MoMo happily towed JoJo around Big Bear Lake, cruising on a boat was fun on this fine, sunny day! And when JoJo took breaks, MoMo dipped into the cool, crystal-clear lake with his snorkeling gear on.

JoJo soon took off for his next mini-adventure of the day, and MoMo found a little rock island to bask on, eventually falling into another signature MoMo-nap while reading a book on a hammock.

JoJo in the Air

As the sun headed fast toward the horizon, JoJo wanted more fun, and what is more fun for a Pup than wind in the face!

Up, up, up in a little airplane went JoJo, his heart thumping and blood pumping, for what he was just about to do! Whooooosh jumped out JoJo! All four limbs spread-eagled into a smooth sky-dive.

In all the excitement of free-falling through the sky, JoJo couldn't help but notice the beautiful golden light from the sunset wash over the little village of Big Bear Lake. "Aight, aight, what a sight!"

MoMo in the Air

JoJo the Pup may have picked the craziest way to experience the last light of day, but MoMo the Tort was also in the air soon, in a nice and slow Hot Air Balloon!

Gliding gently through the brilliantly hued evening sky with no hurry or worry, MoMo enjoyed the view in all its glory: the lit-up village, the vast and still lake, the dark forest, and the sharp snowy peaks now reflecting the last rays of the sun.
"My, my, so soothing to the eye!"

JoJo In the Village

Back on land, JoJo had one last item to check off his bucket list for this trip, so off he went to the little village of Big Bear Lake, and into a Music Concert!

JoJo the Pup was now finally running out of his signature energy, but the night was young and so was he, so he danced, and danced, and danced with glee!

MoMo In the Village

For MoMo, nothing was better than ending the day with a nice soak in a Hot Tub in a cozy little cabin!

Slow music, a hot soak for sore muscles, and a cold drink in hand, "All's well in this Tort's shell!" sighs MoMo, weaving in and out of his signature naps...(zzzzzzzzzzzzzz)...

JoJo & MoMo Call it a Night

Speaking of sore muscles, there's JoJo!

JoJo and MoMo share each other's highlights of the day at Big Bear Lake, including the photographs they took along the way: selfies of sleeping MoMo and leaping JoJo!

So Friend, whether you like to have your adventure like JoJo, or MoMo, or a bit of both, Make sure it is an awesome one!

Goodnight from JoJo & MoMo

MoMo: "As our eyes close under these blinking stars and glowing moon...(zzzzzz)"

JoJo: "...we cannot wait to embark on our next adventure, see you soon!...(zzzzzz)"

JoJo & Momo's favorite quote from their Adventures at Big Bear Lake

JoJo's:

"There's no WiFi in the forest, but you'll find a better connection."

– unknown

MoMo's:

"Take a deep breath. Inhale peace. Exhale happiness."

– A. D. Posey

THE END

About the Author

The author hails from the beautiful East African country of Tanzania, where he spent much of his childhood outdoors in his country's many wildlife parks, forests, mountains and beaches. For this first book about adventures of his beloved pets JoJo the Pup and MoMo the Tortoise, he draws inspiration from his trip to Big Bear Lake in California. Such breaks from the daily grind are medicine for the mind and soul. The author prefers being both "a JoJo" and "a MoMo" on his trips, but usually leans more MoMo! He is an Aerospace Engineer by profession, and dedicates his first children's book to all the kids who read this book and hopefully get out the door to go on adventures, even if it's on a tree-house in their backyard! He lives with his wife and two sons in Southern California.

Made in the USA
Las Vegas, NV
28 December 2024

15385728R00026